HORSE & BUGGY

PLANT A SEED!

HORSE & BUGGY

PLANT A SEED!

Ethan Long

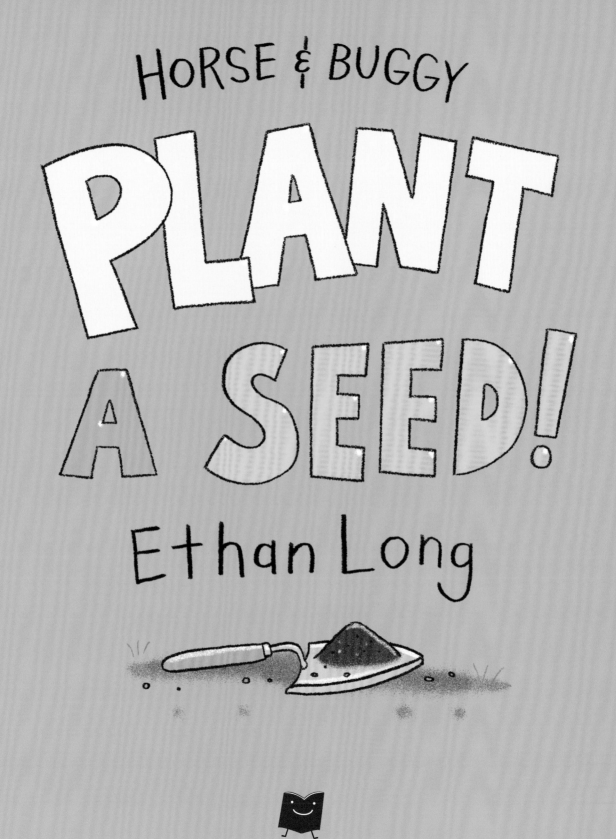

I Like to Read®

HOLIDAY HOUSE • NEW YORK

3 5 7 9 10 8 6 4 2

This book has been officially leveled by using
the F&P Text Level Gradient™ Leveling System.

Library of Congress Cataloging-in-Publication Data
Names: Long, Ethan, author, illustrator.
Title: Horse & Buggy plant a seed! / Ethan Long.
Other titles: Horse and Buggy plant a seed
Description: First edition. | New York : Holiday House, [2020] | Audience:
Ages 4–8. | Audience: Grades K–1. | Summary: After Horse and his friend
Buggy plant a seed, Horse must exercise patience while waiting for it to grow.
Identifiers: LCCN 2019029200 | ISBN 9780823444984 (hardcover)
Subjects: CYAC: Gardening—Fiction. | Seeds—Fiction. | Patience—Fiction
Horses—Fiction. | Carriages and carts—Fiction.
Classification: LCC PZ7.L8453 Hor 2020 | DDC [E]—dc23
LC record available at https://lccn.loc.gov/2019029200

ISBN 978-0-8234-4498-4 (hardcover)
ISBN 978-0-8234-4861-6 (paperback)